For Cameron
— *M.N.D.*

Mary Newell DePalma has written and illustrated a number of children's books, including *Now It Is Summer* (Eerdmans), as well as *A Grand Old Tree* (Scholastic), which received the IRA/CBC Children's Choice award.

Text and Illustrations © 2011 by Mary Newell DePalma

Published in 2011 by Eerdmans Books for Young Readers,
an imprint of Wm. B. Eerdmans Publishing Co.
2140 Oak Industrial Dr. NE, Grand Rapids, Michigan 49505
P.O. Box 163, Cambridge CB3 9PU U.K.

www.eerdmans.com/youngreaders

Manufactured at Tien Wah Press, in Singapore, February 2011, first edition

17 16 15 14 13 12 11   8 7 6 5 4 3 2 1

Library of Congress Cataloging-in-Publication Data

DePalma, Mary Newell.
Uh-oh! / by Mary Newell DePalma.
p. cm.
Summary: A youngster has a series of mishaps
in this nearly wordless picture book.
ISBN 978-0-8028-5372-1 (alk. paper)
[1. Behavior — Fiction. 2. Humorous stories.]
I. Title.
PZ7.D4385Uh 2011
[E] — dc22
2010048403

Uh-oh!

Mary Newell DePalma

Eerdmans Books for Young Readers
Grand Rapids, Michigan • Cambridge, U.K.

Uh-oh!

Ahhhh!

Uh-oh!

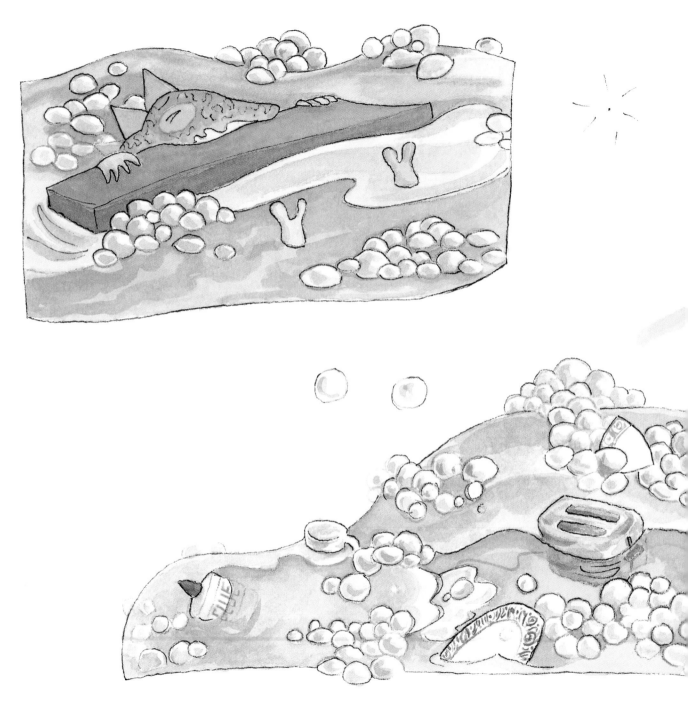

Uh-oh!